The Great Witch Mum

An ever-becoming tale...

Alan Richardson

with

Caroline Jarosz

To Trisha Waters
who also knows
Swinley Topp...

Alan
Richardson

Dedicated to

Margaret. Zoe, Kirsty, Jade and Lara
Marley, Saffi and Erin

&

Richard. Matthias and Josiah

Introduction
&
WARNING!!

This is a **true** story. It is the story of **your** life. In the space of 3,101 words (plus full stops, hesitantly placed semi-colons and some jolly useful commas) it is about you - whether you realise it or not, whether you have children or not. Everything in this tale has already happened to you, is happening, or will happen. The story is ever-becoming, worlds without end.

If you have ever yearned for the Lost Child in the Land of the Ever Young (which is, of course, within your own self), then you will dive beneath these words and swim in the rivers of the windfall light.

You will realise that *you* are the Great Witch Mum and also the Dear Old Dad, whatever your sex, whatever your age, whatever your relationship status.

If you've ever glimpsed that wide-eyed, supple, pure, hopeful and often fearful little mite, then you'll read this and know that this is **your** biography.

Chapter the First and Last

Four little girls lived in a small house, in the narrow street of a tiny village which squatted like a hare upon a high hill known as Swinley Topp. It was a place that was always scraped by clouds and sometimes hooked by rainbows. In the whole terrible history of that hill there had never been four like them.

Others in the village thought that they were nice quiet little girls, who went on nice quiet little walks around the leafy lanes, and did nice quiet little things with dollies and prams and hamsters... but two people at least, knew different. For when the Moon was low and their moods were high, and the wind groaned in the chimney and made the noises of dead men, they gave each other secret nods and wicked looks and became at once *The Four Little Witches!*

The four little witches had amazing powers. By making odd, twisting gestures with their hands and turning their little mouths down, they could make money disappear from Dad's pocket. At least three times a day they made him speechless, gave him headaches and pains in the neck, and used particularly weird and unpleasant spells to get right up his nose. Sometimes he wondered if they could also turn invisible:

"Where have you been?" he would ask, having looked for them everywhere.

"Nowhere!" they would cry, and disappear once more in a flash of light, dragging the witch-baby after them.

Every day, they would turn another of his once-beautiful black hairs grey.

"That's 53 gone grey now" he said glumly, peering into the mirror,

knowing he never stood a chance against them.

Three of the four little witches cackled. "*Poor old Dad!*" they would snigger, but the youngest, who

wore fatwitch nappies and had only 1 candle on her happy witchday cake kissed his knee and said "*Aaaah...* " and he started to melt all over the floor. "*That's a good spell!*" said the others admiringly, scraping him up afterward, and it was a good job it was a stain-resistant carpet.

When the little witches fought, which was often, the whole of Swinley Topp trembled. There might have been earthquakes, or storms, if it hadn't been for their Mum. Others in the village thought she was a nice quiet Mum, who took her nice little girls on those nice little walks when she wasn't making corn dollies, learning aromatherapy or shaving her legs.

But four little witchgirls knew different - and Dad wouldn't have dared say anything anyway. For when their moods were high and her patience low, she made strange grinding noises with her back teeth while muttering powerful words that she was careful not to let anyone else hear, and she became at once...the Great Witch Mum.

Only the Great Witch Mum had more powers

 than they. When they crossed her she could breathe fire, fly up the wall, hit the roof and become a real dragon. She had the power to make their blood run cold, their hair stand on end, and with a snap of her fingers and some odd barking noises she could even get them to tidy their rooms.

"Oooooh..." they said, wincing. But the thirdwitch girl who had three candles in her cake and high bunches like horns, and who had the power to see right through things, called her Dear Old Mum.

On Friday nights, after school, the witches were always impossible. Dear Old Mum and Poor Old Dad, sitting downstairs and trying to watch the X Factor couldn't hear themselves think.

"They must have turned into elephants!" cried Dad, as the pictures shook and shelves rattled and his renowned collection of framed beer mats fell off the wall.

Steam came from the Great Witch Mum's ears. This always happened before she changed, and when she got in a right stew. Three more grey hairs appeared on Poor Old Dad and two more lines under his haunted eyes.

Upstairs:

"Ssssh!" said the oldest, tallest, firstwitch girl, who had ears like a bat and had blown out nine candles on her last cake. "Mummy will come flying up."

"Oh help" said the secondwitch girl, who was 7 and knew everything. "She'll eat us alive and then spew us out. That's what dragons do you know." In a flash four thumping, trumpeting witch elephants turned at once into four little cherubs asleep in their bunks when the Great Witch Mum appeared in their doorway in a right flap, her blood boiling, spitting fire.

"I'll give you four What For in a minute!" as lightnings flashed and thunder shook the uPVC windows, and strong men on distant hills felt glad they didn't have to live on Swinley Topp just then.

"Dear Old Mum" said the thirdwitch sucking her thumb and buried under her dollies, who wasn't afraid of dragons anyway.

"Nuh-night" said the babywitch, sucking her witch-teddy's leg.

T he four little witches could turn things into other things. Bits of old rubbish became... well, anything they wanted. One morning before breakfast the oldest two flew to Mars and back in the laundry basket that they changed into a spaceship, and

turned the kitchen into –

"A right mess!" cried the Great Witch Mum, who wasn't amused that the knickers strewn over the

floor had become Martian jellyfish, or that her best pairs of tights were now life-threatening alien beings.

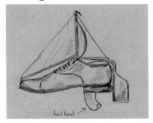 The third little witch turned her dad's best shoes (with real leather uppers) into magic boats and sailed her dollies in them, in the bath.

While the littlest fourthwitch girl made funny cooing noises and turned everyone gooey, and twisted them round her little finger twice a day.

 *"They keep us hopping, this lot do"* said the Dad grimly, when he had a chance to sit down, counting his grey hairs again. *"541, 542,543..."* and rubbing magic creams into a brow that was once milk-smooth if a little low.

Once, when the Gran visited, they had changed Poor Old Dad into a bridge over a shark-infested river, and the sitting room was a desperate and dangerous place to be just then.

"Honestly, they're walking all over him!" said the Gran sourly, wrapping her heavy black coat more firmly around her. She had been a Great Witch Mum

herself once, but had now turned into something of
an Old Crow.

"Oh leave him alone" said the real Great Witch
Mum to her in-law. "He's happy..."

"That's what dads are for" said the secondwitch
girl, wrestling with a mohair jumper that someone
had turned into an octopus.

But the Great Witch Mum showed her greatest
powers and astonished the four little witches
regularly when she turned into a little girl
herself, the wildest of them all, who raced faster,
spit further, yelled louder, danced madly, and who
could turn a few cakes and lemonade into a Royal
Feast at the end of it all.

"That's what Mums can do" said the second little
witch knowingly, tapping the side of her nose and
raising one eyebrow to the sky.

"How can I become like you, Mama?" asked the
oldest, dreamiest witchgirl, who was learning French
and secretly practising snogging on her forearm.

"Believe me" said the Great Witch Mum, tucking
her skirt into her knickers and doing cartwheels up
the garden. "You don't want to know..."

"4,585, 4,586, 4,587 . . ." muttered Poor Old
Dad, looking into his mirror again.

The magic went on and on, grew stronger and stranger. Even the Great Witch Mum herself, for all her powers, was sometimes turned into a Quivering Heap by the things they did.

"*That's dangerous!*" she'd cry, as they became witch-cats and walked along walls, but they made themselves deaf and carried on as witch-cats do.

"*She'll spit feathers now*" purred the first little witch, casting a backward spell. And the Great Witch Mum did exactly that, and there were feathers around the house for weeks afterward, and it took a long time to clean up **that** mess.

And as for Poor Old Dad, well, he spent most of his days being turned into a tizzy, although he couldn't easily have drawn such a thing if you'd asked him. "You little toads!" he'd shout, but they always hopped off, croaking with laughter.

On and on, on and on.....
But there came a day when things started happening to the actual shapes of the two older witches, and to Poor Old Dad's eye it was like a spell of theirs going badly wrong, for they didn't seem like

his little girls at all lately, the way they slouched and mooched about.

"*I'll soon sort this!*" said the Great Witch Mum putting her serious head on and rolling her sleeves up beyond her dimpled elbows. "*Into your bedroom, both of you!*" And while they were getting their Long Talk their old dad (who had smelled this sort of trouble coming on) moped around outside until the door opened and...

"*But you're wearing bras!*" he said in astonishment.

"*Oh Papa!*" said the firstwitch girl storming off. She had persisted with her French over the years, and could now knit, plait her hair, and was learning to kiss in that language.

"That's what puberty does" said the secondwitch girl a little too knowingly, and who briefly turned into a beetroot before following her sister.

 "*They're little witch-women now*" he said glumly, looking at the Great Witch Mum as if it were all her fault, then grabbing the two remaining witchgirls and bouncing them madly on his knees as if they were still babies, and he could call back the years.

But the worst of it all was when the Boys came. These were entirely different creatures to those which had been around when Poor Old Dad had been one himself.  Obviously, they had suffered mutation in the meantime, so that these were closer to rats than anything else. Personally he blamed the atom bomb, lead in the petrol, and the spicy things they put in the food these days, in that order.

 And these ratboys who came around were a real plague. They got everywhere: in the cupboards, under the stairs, in the garden and under the bed... and it was impossible to keep them out of the fridge. He could hardly move without stepping on one of those twitching, cunning, sleek little pests. The whole house - the whole street - was filled with their shuffling and snuffling, squeaking and creaking, with a disturbing undertone of wet snogging noises.

"They're eating us out of house and home!" he wailed. "Do something about them" he pleaded to his witchgirls. So they smiled and turned the ratboys inside-out and upside-down; they made them into chewed string and lumps of jelly. They ate them up and spat them out - but still they came. *"Can't you do something?"* he begged the Great Witch Mum herself, hoping she might have some spell that would drive them all away, or at least get their drool off their doorstep.

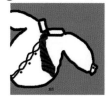 *"Oh you're turning into a real Stuffed Shirt..."* said the Great Witch Mum calmly, who was always better in a crisis.

"15,132 15,133 - " he counted, looking in the mirror, hoping for a Pied Piper but seeing the reflection of the Old Crow instead, coming up the garden path and in a right lather about all the rat-spoor she saw, and the twitching faces at every window.

"What's this?" asked the Old Crow when she settled into her son's favourite armchair and glowered at the Great Witch Mum. *"This place become Boys R Us now has it?"* She croaked, for she hated boys, and was well-known for having tried to turn her son into a worm. Her daughter-in-law said  nothing but gave a tight smile, while wisps of steam gathered at her ears, and claws could he seen

flexing. "And if you ask me them *girls* of yours are turning into little tarts!"

The house went silent. Dad went white as his

 heart went into his mouth and stopped beating. Witchgirls and ratboys turned to stone as an earth tremor shook the world of Swinley Topp and the tarmac peeled back on the roads.

"*I'm sick of you poking your bloody beak in where it isn't wanted!*" roared the Great Witch Mum in her full and dragon glory, saying words that enabled her to jump down the Old Crow's throat, rip her apart, changing her guts for garters, and then sending her home in little pieces.

"*Cor...*" said the littlest witchgirl who had 5 candles now, a bike with only two wheels, and who loved a good fight.

"*Listen*" said the Great Witch Mum, making a sign that caused all the ratboys to scamper off to their own nests, then gathering her little brood under her still-quivering dragon wings.

"*Don't ever let anyone turn you into doormats, no matter how old you get*" she said, coming back to earth again.

"Dear Old Mum" said the thirdwitch girl, putting her dolls aside and proudly kissing her mum on each red and angry cheek, "We'll never fall for that spell!"

One day, much later, when Mum and Dad had lost count of the number of ratboys that had been turned into dishrags and then hung out on the line to dry, the firstwitch girl developed a fever. She couldn't sleep or hardly eat. Her eyes were unnaturally wide and troubled.

"She's caught an illness from those rodents" fumed her Dad, fearing the start of the Great Plague of Swinley Topp. He was about to call an ambulance when the doorbell rang, and he opened it to find a sleek and nervous young ratboy on the step, twitching his whiskers and saying;

"Sir.... I've brought some new and unusual beermats to add to your justly famous collection!"

Poor Old Dad blinked, and accepted the handsome gift while explaining that he had to rush, that his eldest daughter hadn't slept in days and that she was turning into a shadow.

"But that's what happens when you fall in love, Dad" said the secondwitch girl, waving shyly to another ratboy on a mountain-bike outside, who had passed the house a thousand times at least.

"In love?!" said the Dad as if hit by lightning, thunderstruck by the way that the invalid now stood next to him, quivering.

"Je t'adore" said the ratboy, taking her hand in his greasy paw. "You are magic. You enchant me. You keep me under a spell. I am completely bewitched and bewildered..."

"What's he talking about?" asked Poor Old Dad in desperation, for he didn't think that any other male knew about his daughter's powers. "He's cracked. He's turned potty. Why's he saying these things?"

"You used to say things like that" said the Great Witch Mum wistfully, remembering when her husband had had a bit of magic also before he got the wrong end of the magic stick and turned himself into a bit of a cabbage.

"He's still a rat" said the Dad, watching the pair of them walk off hand-in-hand toward the autumn sun.

"55, 56, 57..." said the fourthwitch child, sitting on her dad's chest. as he lay on the floor and let her count his remaining black hairs.

As they got older still the little witches did bizarre things to the hours and minutes.

"But where has all the Time gone?!" said the Dad, fiddling with his clocks and calendars; and the years became weeks, and the weeks became days, and in the all the confusion the firstwitch girl turned into a High Flier and flew to foreign climes, while the second and thirdwitches (who went through phases of becoming little cows for a while) ambled off for the greener pastures of neighbouring hills.

Then Dad might have panicked but the Great Witch Mum, like all Singular Mums, knew it was all just a stage, and they'd all come back again one day. And if the fourthwitch girl was nearly ready to make her own changes and disappear in her own sweetwitch way, then he had to keep his hair on and leave her be.

So there came a moment when the house was quiet. Unbelievably quiet. So quiet you could hear Dad's famous collection of beer mats curling at the edges. And it was a wonder the building had survived at all considering the number of times the Mum had

gone up through the ceiling or Dad fallen down through the floorboards at some new spell - not to mention the times when the four little witches had brought the house down entirely with their magic games.

"I don't like this" said the Dad, picking up another of the black feathers that seemed to be falling from his wife these days. The Mum said nothing but carried on knitting hard, sending sparks flying across the room and singeing the once-splendid, formerly stain-proof carpet of another Age. "They're around somewhere" he added, "I just know it. They're making my ears burn again." Which, of course, was the oldest spell in their much-used book. "4, 3, 2, 1..." he finished, plucking out the remaining black hairs, knowing when he was beaten at last.

A key turned in the lock. Slowly, slowly, the door opened. *"Happy Anniversary!"* came a cry, and suddenly his little witches (who of course were now taller and straighter than he) were all over him again, and still with enough power to make his eyes water.

"Oh my, look at you all, together again at last..." he said, remembering when he could bounce them all on his knee at the same time. *"You're women now, not my little girls at all. There's no going back, you can't change **this** spell."*

"Oh leave them alone!" squawked his wife, looking eagerly toward the open door and little wobbling shadow beyond. *"Be happy. They're happy!"*

"But five minutes ago they were just little girls and I had black hair. Now look at them." he said, and there was something wrong with this voice, they'd put some sort of a lump in his throat.

"But Dad look!" they cried, waving their hands and working one more spell. And in through the door marched a single little tot in her fatwitch nappy, just ready to start turning things into other things, and twist big people round her podgy little fingers.

"Gosh, you've turned us into grandparents overnight!" said the oldest couple, reaching out to the baby and the start of a whole new spell.

"Dear Old Mum, Dear Old Dad" said the firstwitch Great Witch Mum and her auntwitch sisters together.

Some other books by Alan Richardson:

Aleister Crowley and Dion Fortune

The Inner Guide to Egypt with Billie Walker-John (various editions)

Priestess - the Life and Magic of Dion Fortune (various editions)

The Magician's Tables (utter tosh)

The Magical Kabbalah (more tosh – but numerous editions in several languages)

The Google Tantra - How I became the First Geordie to raise the Kundalini

Sex and Light – how to Google your way to Godhood (new edition of above; autobiography)

The Old Sod with Marcus Claridge

Spirits of the Stones

Inner Guide to the Megaliths. (Later edition of above)

Spirits of the Stones Revisited

Earth God Rising - the Return of the Male Mysteries

Earth God Risen

Letters of Light

Gate of Moon

Dancers to the Gods

Ancient Magick with Geoff Hughes. (largely tosh)

Inner Celtia. with David Annwn

Plus the Prologomenon (whatever that is) to the new edition of Robert Kirk's 1691 classic The Secret Commonwealth   Mandrake 2006

Fiction

The Giftie

On Winsley Hill

The Fat Git – the story of a Merlin

Dark Light

Du Lac

The Movie Star – When Dorset Swallowed Hollywood

Shimmying Hips (Illustrated) – a Tale of Magick, Sex and Football

Website (currently frozen, though I'm buggered if I can understand why):

www.alric.pwp.blueyonder.co.uk
email: *alric@blueyonder.co.uk*